Côte d'Azur, France

New York
Public Library

This book is for all of my FRIENDS. XO, K

to my editor, Jill— You are better than imported sardines!

SARDINES

HarperCollins
PUBLISHERS
Since 1817

Mr. Biddles
Copyright © 2017 by Kristine A. Lombardi
All rights reserved. Manufactured in China.

ISBN 978-0-06-244114-0

The art in this book was created with pencil, gouache, brayer & ink, collage, old bits of ledgers, receipts, airmail envelopes, random
objects from desk drawers, little bits scavenged in antique barns, snapped photos I knew I'd put to use one day (but no idea where I'd use
them until this book was born), and countless cups of coffee while I worked. Every element was then meticulously assembled in Photoshop.

Typography by Rachel Zegar   17 18 19 20 21 SCP 10 9 8 7 6 5 4 3 2 1   ❖   First Edition

Mr. Biddles

Kristine A. Lombardi

HARPER
An Imprint of HarperCollinsPublishers

Meet Mr. Biddles.

He's an inventor who lives alone
in that house up on the hill.

All that peace and quiet helps him focus on his work.

It gets lonesome at times,

but he stays busy.

Mr. Biddles was working one day when the doorbell rang.

"Who are you?" asked Mr. Biddles.

"My name is Hobson. I was minding my own business, sitting in a kelp cluster, when I was plucked from the ocean and shipped off."

"That's awful!" said Mr. Biddles, snipping the rubber bands from Hobson's claws. "I was just in the middle of something. You can come to the lab— but please, don't touch anything."

Mr. Biddles got back to work on his catnip diffuser when a washer fell off. Without thinking, Hobson grabbed it in his right claw and handed it to Mr. Biddles.

KEEP OUT

While others would just see
two lobster claws, Mr. Biddles
saw a gold mine of possibilities!

"I can't believe it!" cried Mr. Biddles.
"You are the extra set of hands I've
always needed!"

wrench

vise

bolt holder

gripper

ratchet

OUCH!

Soon Hobson had his own lab coat and two-story tricked-out tank.

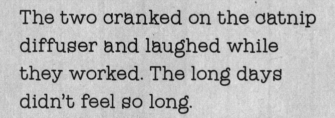

The two cranked on the catnip diffuser and laughed while they worked. The long days didn't feel so long.

At night they made plankton popcorn and watched Hobson's favorite show on the Crustacean Network.

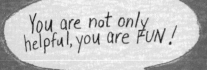

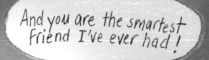

One day in the lab when Mr. Biddles asked Hobson to pass a washer, he got a hex bolt instead.

That night at dinner, Hobson's smile had faded. He was hardly eating.

"I miss my family," he said.

Mr. Biddles couldn't sleep that night. It seemed clear—his little buddy was homesick. But how could he get him home?

They tried everything, but Hobson couldn't be out of water for long. They had to come up with a better plan.

Not everyone wanted passengers with five gallons of water splashing everywhere.

Mr. Biddles devised a plan. The next day, the usual levers, pulleys, and springs were replaced with algae, sand, and sealant. "Just what are we making anyway?" Hobson asked.

"You'll see soon enough, my friend."

"Presenting the Super Lobster Sightseeing Sidecar!"

"Yippee!" yelled Hobson. "Are we really going to Maine?"

The two finally made it! Hobson's family was overjoyed to see him again. They planned a giant clambake on the beach.

They roasted marshmallows, played five rounds of Flip the Mollusk,

and laughed until the moon fell behind the dunes.

The next morning, they had potato sack races on the beach.

Mr. Biddles watched Hobson's family having fun from his bedroom window. How could he tell Hobson it was almost time to leave? He couldn't.

So Mr. Biddles unpacked Hobson's suitcase, wrote a note . . .

WELCOME ON BOARD

Dear Hobson,
You belong here with your family.
I will visit you. ♡,
MR. B

Three long weeks passed, but it felt like three years. Watching TV at night without Hobson by his side was nowhere near as fun.

The lab was not the same
without those magical claws.

Even his imported
sardines tasted dull.

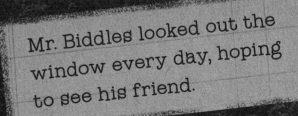

Mr. Biddles looked out the window every day, hoping to see his friend.

Then one evening, everything in his lab began to shake, jiggle, and bounce. There was a loud noise coming from above the house.

automated slipper fetcher

He ran outside to see what it was.

And there was the most wonderful sight
Mr. Biddles had ever seen—better than any
invention, better than any tasty sardine, even
better than the beautiful coast of Maine.

It was his very best friend in the world.
And he was back for good.

Coney Island

Newburyport, Ma.

Woonsocket, RI